FLASH
THE LITTLE FIRE ENGINE

By PAM CALVERT
Illustrated by JEN TAYLOR

two lions

Published by Two Lions, New York

www.apub.com

Amazon, the Amazon logo, and Two Lions are trademarks of
Amazon.com, Inc., or its affiliates.

ISBN-13: 9781542041782 (hardcover)
ISBN-10: 1542041783 (hardcover)

The illustrations are rendered in digital media.

Book design by AndWorld Design
Printed in China

First Edition

10 9 8 7 6 5 4 3 2 1

RING! RING!

To my little firefighters, Hunter and T. Rex. I love you!
—P. C.

To Marc and my family
—J. T.

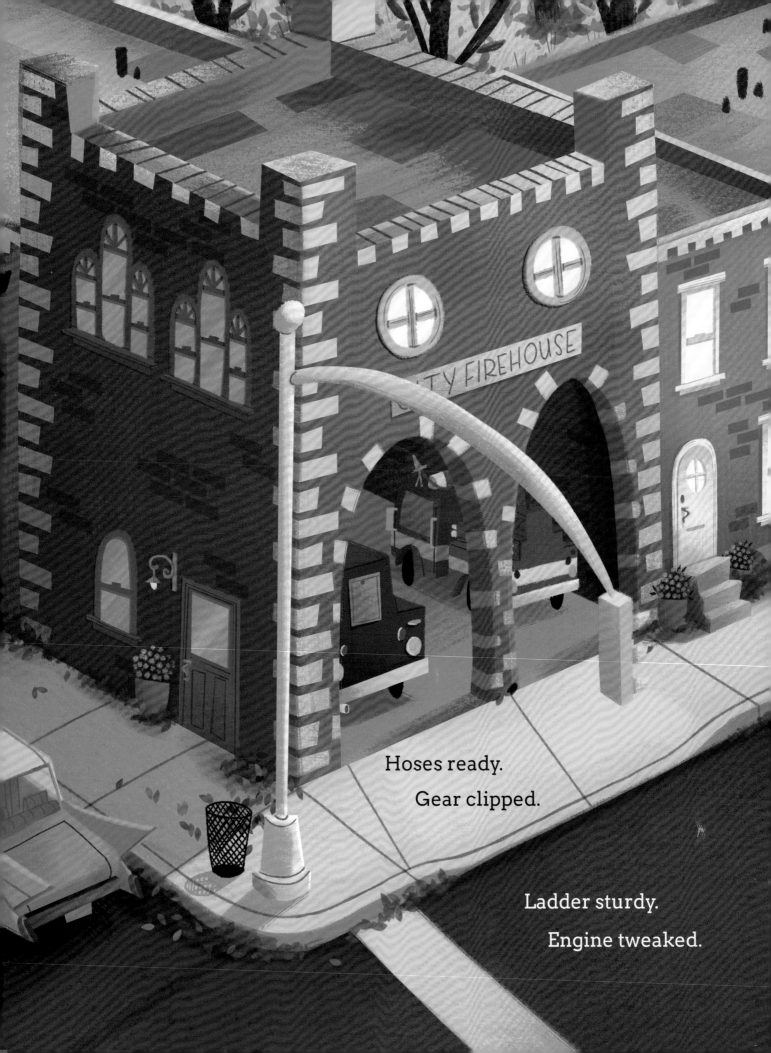

Hoses ready.

Gear clipped.

Ladder sturdy.

Engine tweaked.

I'M **FLASH** THE LITTLE FIRE ENGINE, READY FOR THE DAY!

Chief says I'm big enough now to help our town!
And today is my very first day on the job.

I rumble through the square to celebrate.
The people wave and smile.
I beep a loud hello.

No emergencies! All is well.

But when I come back to the firehouse . . .

RRRING!

RRRING!

Oh no!

Alert!
Alert!

The firefighters **WHOOSH** down the pole.

They slip on their gear.

I'm on my way. I'll save the day!

A fire at the airport!
I see the blaze plume as it roars like thunder.

My friend Crash is an
airport crash tender.

**"TOO BIG FOR YOU,
LITTLE BUDDY,"** she says.

Crash goes to work, spraying foam on the blaze.

Now the fuel won't explode.

The fire is out! The people are saved!

FIZZ!

FIZZ!

I roll back to the station.
Maybe next time I can help?

Fire ahead!
I see smoke billowing from a tall building.

"TOO TALL FOR YOU, LITTLE FLASH," my friend Laddie says. He's a turntable ladder truck, made to reach high places. He cranks his ladder all the way to the top.

SMASH! go the windows. **WHOOSH!** thunders the water.

The fire is out!
The people are saved!

I drive back to the station.
I'll help next time.

RRRING! RRRING!

WARNING!
WARNING!

The firefighters hurry.

"GOT THE CHAINSAW?
AND THE POLES?"

YES! It's all stowed in my side compartment.

I'm on my way! I'll save the day!

The forest is on fire!
I'd better roll fast!
My engine **THRUMS** as I speed toward the blaze.

Before I can reach the forest,
I see Tank the airplane firefighter
up high in the sky.

He drops a blanket of flame retardant
over the area.

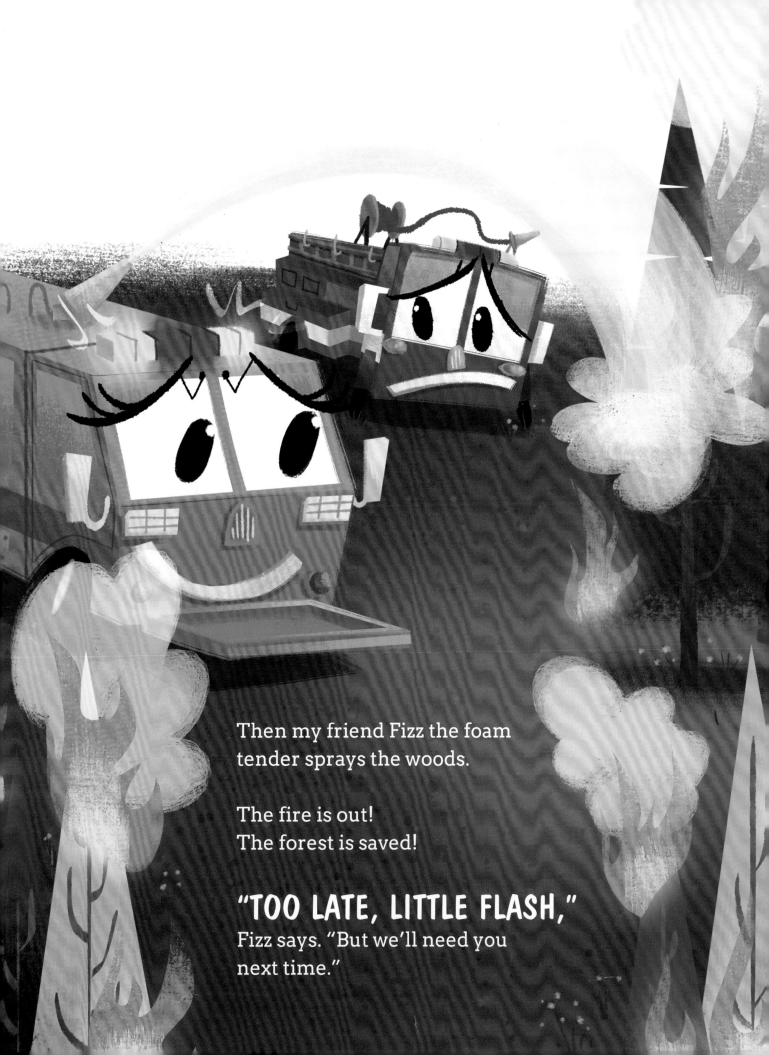

Then my friend Fizz the foam
tender sprays the woods.

The fire is out!
The forest is saved!

"TOO LATE, LITTLE FLASH,"
Fizz says. "But we'll need you
next time."

Tires slow. Engine throbs.
Should I go back to the station?

**MAYBE FIZZ IS WRONG.
NO ONE SEEMS TO NEED ME.**

Cold wind picks up. Flurries form.
Sleet plinks my windows.
I shiver in the night, rolling slowly
over the icy streets.

"Flash! Where are you?"
the chief hollers over my speakers.

"I'm still on the other side of town," I explain.

"The bridge is blocked with snow," the chief says.
"We can't get through right now. There's a fire
in the town square! Can you go?"

Could this be true?
No time to lose!

I rush through the slippery snow
to the town square.
IT'S THE ANIMAL SHELTER!
OH NO!

My hoses spray! My axes crash!

Smoke billows. Fire flickers out of the windows.

Can I help the animals? Can I help the people?

The fire is out!

The animals are rescued!

Workers are saved!

I roll back to the station,
dirty and tired. But when I arrive . . .

HOORAY FOR LITT

...there's a celebration!

Then it's off to bed for me.

Gear unhooked.

Hoses stored.

Chrome polished.

Lights out.

I smile inside as my engine *HUMS* itself to sleep.

I'M FLASH THE LITTLE FIRE ENGINE,
READY FOR THE DAY!